Edwardo

The Horriblest Boy in the Whole Wide World

John Burningham

Alfred A. Knopf · New York

For Tiny Tom

THIS IS A BORZOI BOOK PUBLISHED BY ALFRED A. KNOPF

Published in the United States by Alfred A. Knopf, an imprint of Random House Children's Books, a division of Random
House, Inc., New York. Originally published in Great Britain by Jonathan Cape, an imprint of Random House Children's
Books, in 2006.

KNOPF, BORZOI BOOKS, and the colophon are registered trademarks of Random House, Inc.

www.randomhouse.com/kids

Educators and librarians, for a variety of teaching tools, visit us at www.randomhouse.com/teachers

Library of Congress Cataloging-in-Publication Data
Burningham, John.
Edwardo : the horriblest boy in the whole wide world / John Burningham. — 1st American ed.
p. cm.
SUMMARY: Each time he does something a little bit bad, Edwardo is told that he is very bad and soon his behavior is awful,
but when he accidentally does good things and is complimented, he becomes much, much nicer.
ISBN 978-0-375-84053-1 (trade)
ISBN 978-0-375-94053-8 (lib. bdg.)
[1. Behavior—Fiction. 2. Interpersonal relations—Fiction.] I. Title.
PZ7.B936Edw 2007
[E]—dc22
2006003681

MANUFACTURED IN MALAYSIA

10 9 8 7 6 5 4 3 2

First American Edition

Edwardo was an ordinary boy.

He would get up in the morning,
get dressed, have his breakfast,
go to school, play games,
eat his supper, and go to bed.

Sometimes Edwardo would kick things.

"You are a rough boy, Edwardo. You are always kicking things. You are the roughest boy in the whole wide world." Edwardo became rougher and rougher.

Like most children, Edwardo made a lot of noise.

"You are a very noisy boy, Edwardo. You are the noisiest boy in the whole wide world."
Edwardo became noisier and noisier.

From time to time, Edwardo was nasty to little children.

"You are a nasty bully, Edwardo. You are the nastiest boy in the whole wide world."
Edwardo became nastier and nastier.

Occasionally Edwardo was not very nice to animals and would chase the cat.

"You are a cruel boy, Edwardo, chasing the cat.
You are the cruelest boy in the whole wide world."
Edwardo became more and more cruel.

Edwardo was not always good at keeping his room tidy.

"Your room gets messier and messier every day,
Edwardo. You are the messiest boy in the whole
wide world."
Edwardo's room became messier and messier.

Often Edwardo would forget to wash his face and brush his teeth in the mornings.

"You are a dirty boy, Edwardo. You are the dirtiest boy in the whole wide world."

Edwardo became dirtier and dirtier.

And as the days turned into weeks and the weeks into months, Edwardo became even clumsier, crueler, noisier, messier, dirtier, nastier, ruder, and rougher until one day they said . . .

"Edwardo, you really are

THE HORRIBLEST BOY

IN THE WHOLE WIDE WORLD."

Then one day, when Edwardo kicked a pot of flowers, it flew through the air and landed on some earth.

"I see you are starting a little garden, Edwardo. It looks lovely. You should get some more plants."

Edwardo was good at growing things, and he was asked to help people with their gardens.

Cruel Edwardo was waiting for the dog with a bucket of water. He threw it over the dog as it came by.

"Thank you so much, Edwardo, for washing my muddy dog for me. You are so good with animals."

And so Edwardo was asked to clean and look after everybody's pets.

Edwardo's room was getting so untidy that he could not find anything, so he threw everything out of the window.

All Edwardo's things landed in a truck that was collecting for poor people.

"Thank you, Edwardo, for giving all of your things away."

"Look at Edwardo's room. Why can't you all be as neat and tidy as he is?"

Edwardo was becoming dirtier and dirtier until one day he became so dirty that flies started to chase him down the road. He jumped into the river to get away from them.

A lady pulled Edwardo out of the river and took him back to her house. She gave him a hot bath, washed and ironed all his clothes, and sent him back to school.

"Look, children. Look at Edwardo. He is the cleanest and smartest boy in the whole school."

One day at school,
nasty Edwardo pushed
little Alec very hard.

At that moment,
one of the lights
in the room
crashed down
onto the spot
where Alec had
been standing.

"You have just saved
our little Alec. What a
quick-thinking boy you
are. You should look
after the little ones."

And from then on, Edwardo looked after the little children.

One day Edwardo was making more noise than he had ever made before, which frightened some lions who had escaped.

They were so frightened by noisy Edwardo that they went back to their cage.

"You're very good with lions, Edwardo. Perhaps you could come and help me."

Now, from time to time, Edwardo is a little untidy,
cruel, dirty, messy, clumsy, noisy, nasty, and rude.
But really Edwardo is . . .

THE NICEST BOY
IN THE WHOLE
WIDE WORLD.

Edwardo, the horriblest boy in the whole

poijka in den hel jörden Edwardo, el pe

おぞましい おとこのこ एडवर्डो, दुनिया का सबसे शैता

monde Εδουάρδος, το πιο φοβερό αγόρι σ

più orribile del mondo 에드와르드 세상에서

Junge auf der ganzen weiten Welt Эдуа

Edwardo, de verschrikkelijkste jongen in de

chłopak na chłym świecie Edwardo, m

エドワルド せかいで いちばん おぞましい おとこの

wide world Edwardo, le garçon le plus horri

σε ολόκληρο τον κόσμο Edwardo, el peor

Edwardo, najstraszniejszy chłopak na

jongen in de hele wijde wereld 에드와르드 세

orribile del mondo Эдуардо-самый у

schrecklichste Junge auf der ganzen we

エドワルド せかいで いちばん おぞましい おとこの

wide world एडवर्डो, दुनिया का सबसे शैतान लड़का

τον κόσμο Edwardo, il ragazzo più orribi